Dedication

To those who knew me before I was "anybody"
in writing, and whose encouragement helped
change that:

Aileen Andres Sox
(who published my first children's story),
Chris Blake,
Barbara Jackson-Hall,
Richard Coffen,
Kermit Netteburg,
Cec Murphey,
Elaine Grove,
and my brother, David.

At least now, everyone will know who to blame.

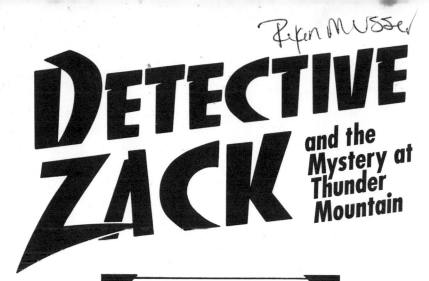

DETECTIVE ZACK

and the Mystery at Thunder Mountain

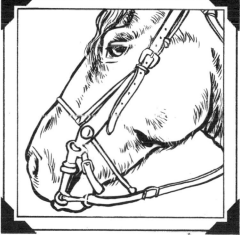

JERRY D. THOMAS

Pacific Press Publishing Association
Boise, Idaho
Oshawa, Ontario, Canada

Pikon Mussed

Edited by Glen Robinson
Designed by Dennis Ferree
Cover and inside art by Kim Justinen
Typeset in 13/16 New Century Schoolbook

Library of Congress Cataloging-in-Publication Data:

Thomas, Jerry D., 1959-
    Detective Zack and the Mystery at Thunder Mountain / Jerry
D. Thomas.
        p.   cm.
    Summary: Zack investigates the mystery of disappearing
items and unusual nighttime activities at Thunder Mountain
Camp, while pondering what it means to be a Christian.
    ISBN 0-8163-1212-5
    [1. Camps. 2. Christian life. 3. Mystery and detective stories.]
I. Title. II. Series: Thomas, Jerry D., 1959-   . Detective Zack ;
4.
PZ7.T366954De   1994
[Fic]—dc20   93-41480
                                                                  CIP
                                                                  AC

95 96 97 98 ● 5 4 3

Contents

CHAPTER ONE

Thunder Mountain Camp

Day One

A pencil doesn't make a very good fly swatter. I've been trying to swat a mosquito with this one, but I keep missing.

I'm lying in one of the top bunks of the Cherokee cabin at Thunder Mountain Camp. Writing in this cabin while the other guys are shouting and throwing pillows isn't easy, I can tell you.

While I was unrolling my sleeping bag, Luke, one of the other Cherokees, climbed up on the next bunk. "Is this your first year at Thunder Mountain Camp?" He went on before I could answer. "I was here last year. We had a great time."

I like Luke already. He laughs a lot. "What are

the horses like? My mom signed me up for horse-back riding, and I'm not sure I like horses," I said.

Before he could answer, there was a loud smack against the other side of the wall. Then we heard loud, rude laughing. "What are they doing in there, tearing up the bunkbeds for firewood?" Luke asked. He threw his hands up and shook his dark black hair. "Those Mohawks! I knew they would be trouble as soon as I saw them."

"Who?" I asked, as the hooting and shouting next door continued.

Peter, who was unrolling his sleeping bag on another bunk, explained, "The Mohawks are the other half of this camp house. Every camp house has two cabins." He counted on his fingers as he talked. "The Cherokees and the Mohawks, the Comanches and Arapaho, the Hopi and the Sioux, and the rest."

Max joined us at my bunk. "And the Mohawks are the worst of the bunch. Did you know they already broke a light in the bathroom, ran one of the Arapaho's hats up the flagpole, and teased one of the Hopi girls so much she wants to go home?"

"Who are those guys?" I asked. No one had an answer for that. But Peter had another question.

"Isn't it time to eat yet?" Just then, the dinner

bell started bonging. Peter was the first one to the door.

The food looked good. Peter's plate was piled high. We sat at a table with some of the Hopi girls, including my sister, Kayla. Pastor Mike asked the blessing and then we dove in.

"Oh, yuck!" A voice called out over the noise of the cafeteria. We all turned to see a tall kid with red hair staring at the food in the serving line. "You call this food?"

Kayla slapped her fork down into her mashed potatoes. Gravy splattered on Luke, but she didn't notice. "That guy makes me so mad!" she said, with clenched teeth. She pointed her fork at me. "He's the one who made Holli cry."

I helped Luke wipe the gravy off his arm. "What did he do that was so mean?" I asked.

Kayla's friend, Ally, answered. "He heard her name when she arrived. After her parents were gone, he started saying, 'Hopi Holli! Dopey, Hopi Holli! Are all the Hopi's as dopey as you?'"

Luke and I just looked at her. "OK," she finally added, "I know it sounds silly to you, but this is her first time away from home, and she was already scared."

Suddenly, a loud whistle almost broke our eardrums. Everyone turned to look. "Attention, campers." It was Mrs. Carter, the camp director. "Welcome to Thunder Mountain Camp. This week is going to be full of fun. You're going to learn to do things you've always wanted to do. But more importantly, you're going to learn more about God."

I was glad to hear that. Because I have questions about God.

Mrs. Carter went on. "You're going to find that the counselors are here to help you learn and have fun. And you already know how good the food is!"

"Yaay!" Some of the kids cheered and clapped. Kayla looked at me. "It's not as good as Mom's food," she whispered.

"Booo!" It was the red-haired boy and his friends. Mrs. Carter looked at them and said, "I'd like you all to meet someone. Mr. Morgan, please come out and say hello to the campers."

The door to the kitchen swung out. A man stepped up and ducked through the doorway. A big black beard covered most of his face, and the black hair on his head stuck out from under his hat. The whole cafeteria got very quiet.

"Campers, I'd like you to meet Mr. Morgan. He's our camp cook." Mr. Morgan waved at us with a long butcher knife and grunted.

Mrs. Carter spoke again. "Mr. Morgan only has two rules about his food. Would you share those with us?"

Mr. Morgan stood up straighter. His head nearly touched the wooden beams. "Number One," he growled, "take all you want, but eat all you take. Number Two, don't complain about it. If you don't like it, just don't eat it." He stared around the room for a minute, then stalked back into the kitchen.

Red-hair and his friends sunk halfway under their table. Kayla took another bite and whispered, "I like this food fine."

Mrs. Carter went on. "You'll be taking classes in horseback riding, canoeing, swimming, tracks and trails, and crafts. Also, each cabin will be performing a scene from the Bible at campfire. Your counselors will be explaining more about this later."

Campfire that evening didn't last long because they knew that everyone needed to get settled and get to sleep. Luke and I were tiptoeing back from the bathroom, trying to walk silently like real Indians did. We froze when the door of the Mohawk cabin flew open. Alan, one of the Mohawks, stuck his head out. "Where is the [he used a curse word] trash can, anyway?" he grumbled.

Then he just dumped the trash on the ground.

Back at our side of the cabin, we had some questions for our counselor, Dave. "What are those Mohawks doing at this camp?"

Dave stretched his tall body across two of the bunks and pretended to get comfortable. He closed his eyes and asked, "What makes you think they don't belong here?"

Everyone tried to talk at once. "They are rude and mean!"

"I heard them cussing."

"I saw cigarettes in one of their bags."

"Cody told me he's been in jail before. He said he burned down a building."

"He was lying. He always lies."

Dave sat up and waved his arms until we stopped. "So you don't think they fit in at a Christian camp?"

"No way!" Luke answered for all of us.

Just then, thunder crashed outside. Only, it wasn't raining. In fact, the stars and moon were shining brightly. "What was that?" Dave asked. He jumped to the door and looked out. We rushed to the windows.

"It sounded like it came from down there," Luke said, pointing into the darkness, "down by the cafeteria."

"I'll be back," Dave said. "You guys stay in the cabin," he called as he disappeared.

"What do you think it was?" Luke whispered.

I had been thinking about that. "Our trash cans at home make noise like that when you crash them together. But why would someone be getting in the trash?"

While we waited for Dave, I was thinking about what he said. About the Mohawks. It reminded me of why I'm writing in my notebook this time.

It all started when I got back from my trip to Egypt and Israel. I had two notebooks full of clues about the Bible and stuff, and . . .

"What'cha writin'?" Luke asked.

Before I could answer, every light in the camp went out.

CHAPTER TWO

Mystery in the Dark

Day Two

It was completely dark. I mean, there was no light anywhere. I waved my hand in front of my eyes, and I couldn't see it. For a second, everyone was silent. Then everyone was talking.

"What's going on?"

"Ouch! I hit my head."

"Get off me!"

"Wait," I shouted. "Everyone stand still. Luke, isn't your flashlight hooked to your belt?"

"Oh, yeah." We could hear Luke fumbling with the light. Then we heard another sound. A stick snapped right outside the door!

"What was that?" Luke whispered. Everyone else was silent again. Then we heard the door creaking open.

"Turn on your light," I hissed at Luke. But

before he did, a voice spoke.

"Hey, are you guys OK?" It was Dave.

We hit him with pillows and questions. "What are you doing sneaking in on us?"

Max sounded tough. "Are you trying to get hurt?"

Before he could tell us anything, the lights came back on. "All right, let's get back to our bunks," Dave announced. "That's enough excitement for one evening."

Max called out from his corner. "So, what was that noise?"

"Yeah, what is going on?" Peter asked. He seemed really worried about the cafeteria.

Dave shook his head. "Some of the trash cans were knocked over. And then for no reason, someone pulled the switch that shuts off electricity to the camp lights."

I started thinking like a detective. "How many people know where that switch is?" I asked.

Dave's eyebrows went up for a second. Then he shrugged. "Who knows? We'll worry about it tomorrow. Now, let's hit the sack."

"Don't you mean the bag?" Luke asked. "You know, the sleeping bags?" Everyone groaned. Max threw a pillow at him.

"But you didn't finish telling us about those

Mohawks," Brian reminded Dave.

Dave nodded. "When everyone is in bed, I'll go on." He waited for a few seconds while Luke emptied three rocks, two sticks of gum, and two quarters out of his pockets.

"OK," Dave said, sitting down beside Brian, "they aren't Christians. Those guys are from a big city. They have never been to a camp. I'm not sure they've ever been to a church! But every summer, we like to bring in kids who especially need the chance to spend time out in nature. And a chance to learn something about God."

We couldn't argue with that. They definitely needed some kind of help.

"Anyway," Dave went on, "they'll learn about horses and canoes and stuff. But a lot of what they learn will depend on you guys."

"What?" I asked.

"A lot of what they learn about Christianity will come from watching Christians—you guys, the counselors, everyone here who claims to be a friend of Jesus."

That gave me a lot to think about. That's kind of what this notebook's all about this time. Last year, I didn't get to go to camp because my dad had to go to a class out in Utah, and the whole family went along. Of course, I learned a lot

17

about Noah's flood on that trip.

My friend, Bobby, thought that the story of Noah's flood and all the stories of the Bible were just fairy tales. But when I told him all the clues I had found on our trip to Utah, he said, "OK. Maybe the flood really did happen."

And when I told him about the things I saw on my trip to Egypt and Israel with Dad and Dr. Doone, he was impressed. He said, "Wow! Maybe the stories in the Bible are true. And God really does help people." He seemed happy to know that.

But the next day, he wasn't smiling. "I talked to my dad about the Bible being true and everything," he told me. "Dad said, 'Ha! Most of the trouble I have at the shop is with Christians. (His dad fixes cars.) They're always trying to cheat me out of my money. If the Bible is true, then people who say they believe in it should be good people. And from what I've seen, they aren't.' "

I didn't know what to say. I think Bobby's dad is right. If the Bible is true, then people who believe in it ought to be different from people who don't. They ought to be more kind and caring. Believing in God should change the way they act.

So, this summer, I'm going to watch for clues that Christians really do act differently. Or clues that they don't.

I was still thinking about all that when I fell asleep. The next thing I knew, someone was screaming in my ear!

I jumped up, but it was just barely light, and everyone else was still asleep. Just when I decided it must have been a dream, it happened again.

"Screeeak!" It was a blue jay sitting in a tree right outside my window.

"Go away!" I said. Then I covered my head with my pillow. I guess I went back to sleep. The next thing I heard was a trumpet.

Really, it was a recording coming from the loudspeaker at the cafeteria. I crawled farther down into my sleeping bag.

A voice followed the trumpet. "Good morning, campers. It's time to rise and shine!"

"It's still nighttime," a voice from Luke's bed said. "I don't want to get up with the chickens."

The loudspeaker voice continued. "Fall out for flag raising in forty minutes."

"Why must we get up so early?" a voice asked.

"You heard Dave last night," I mumbled. "We have to stand at the flagpole and say the pledge of allegiance before breakfast."

"Breakfast! Did someone say breakfast?" Peter swung out of his bunk and snapped on the lights.

DETECTIVE ZACK

"Let's get rolling, Cherokees."

After that, there was no use trying to sleep. While we were getting dressed, Luke started searching around his bed. "Where's my money?" he asked. "I know I had two quarters last night. I put them right here with my gum and rocks."

"I remember seeing them," Brian said. We all did. But now, they were gone.

Luke spun around and looked at all of us. "All right, funny joke. Now, who's got my quarters?"

Everyone shook their heads. Luke rolled his eyes. "So someone snuck in here in the middle of the night and stole my two quarters? I don't think so. I think one of you has them."

Just then, the Mohawks walked past our windows, shouting at each other. Cody's red hair was waving in a friendly way as if it were trying to make up for the scowl on his unfriendly face. "I think it was one of them," Brian whispered.

"Maybe you're right," Luke said with a frown. None of us liked the idea of Mohawks sneaking into our cabin at night. "Come on," he sighed, "let's go before we're late."

I left the cabin last, and took a close look at the door. Could someone sneak in? I guess so! The door didn't even have a lock on it! I started working on a plan.

Clues About Christians

If the Bible is true, then people who believe in it ought to be different from people who don't. They ought to be kinder and more caring. Believing in God ought to change the way people act.

Thunder Mountain Mystery Clues

Some people were out running around the camp. They knocked down the cafe trash cans.

For some reason, the camp lights were all switched off.

Someone snuck into our cabin and took two quarters.

CHAPTER THREE

Mohawk Trouble

Day Two

At the flagpole, we found out that we were supposed to do more than just stand there. We had to stand in line, at attention! Mrs. Carter made us wait that way until everyone was standing properly.

Of course, it was the Mohawks who took so long. "What is this, the army?" Cody grumbled.

Then the Navahos raised the flag. I'm sure the red, white, and blue looked awesome up in the early morning sky. But with all that bright morning light, I had a hard time getting my eyes open far enough to see.

"Hi, guys!" Kayla bounced up and plopped her tray onto our table at breakfast. I grunted at her. Ally sat down too. She stared at me.

"When does your brother wake up?" she asked

Kayla. Like I wasn't even there.

"Usually by lunch time," Kayla laughed.

"Cut the funny stuff, girls," I said. "We've got problems." I told them about our night at the cabin. About the trash cans.

"We heard that noise too," Kayla said.

"And what happened to the lights?" Ally asked.

"We don't know. I want to look around for clues today," I said. "But I don't know when. I've got horse class, then crafts, then canoeing. Maybe I'll have time after supper."

Ally sighed. "I want to look too. But the Hopi cabin is on kitchen duty this morning. That means we have to clean up this mess." She stabbed the eggs on her plate.

"And we get to work with that delightful, happy, smiling Mr. Morgan," Kayla added. Almost as if he had heard her, Mr. Morgan stepped out of the kitchen and glanced around the dining room. Scowling, he went back inside.

"We'd better hurry back for inspection," Luke reminded me. "The others are already gone."

"See you later," I said to the girls after swallowing the last of my orange juice, "maybe at supper." On the way up the hill, I was thinking about Mr. Morgan. Why was he so grumpy and mean-sounding? If he was supposed to be a Christian, he sure didn't act much like one.

As we got close to the cabin, we heard shouting. "Look at this mess! I'm not cleaning it up. It's their trash."

Max, Peter, and Brian were standing in our cabin yard. In front of them on the ground were candy bar and gum wrappers, a banana peel, and some other papers. Max was still shouting.

"We already cleaned up our side of the cabin yard. Then we went in to make our bunks. Now look at this!"

Luke nudged me. "Isn't that the trash Alan was dumping out on the ground last night?"

I nodded. "They pushed all their trash over to our side of the yard, so we would have to pick it up."

"Well, we're not going to do it," Max declared. "We'll just push it back."

A voice called from the corner of the building. "Hey, keep your trash out of our yard." Cody, Alan, and two other Mohawks were standing there.

Max went right over to them. "You know this is not our trash. We know you put it on our side. Now pick it up, or we'll just throw it all back."

"We're not touching it. And anyone who throws trash in our yard gets it." He punched his hand with his fist in case anyone didn't understand what they would get.

Luke spoke up. "Let's just get Dave and tell him what they did. Then they will be the ones who fail inspection."

I was trying to decide whether to go with Max's idea or Luke's when I saw what Brian was doing. He was picking up the trash.

Max saw him too. "Brian! It's not our trash."

"We don't have to pick it up," Luke added.

Brian looked at us. "Remember what Dave said last night?" he said quietly. "About them?" He nodded toward the Mohawks.

I understood what he meant. About the Mohawks not being Christians. And watching the rest of us. And what they would learn.

I started helping Brian pick up trash.

Cody said, "Good idea, Brain."

"His name is Brian," I stated.

Cody laughed. "Whatever. Just keep your trash out of our yard." The Mohawks disappeared around the corner, but we could hear them laughing.

Max was so mad he was shaking. But he took some deep breaths and started helping. So did Luke. Max said, "Being a Christian is harder than I thought."

My first class this morning was the horse class. Mom had told me some long name for it, but I figured the point was learning to ride a horse. Luke and I were walking by the Hopi cabin on our way to the corral when Kayla and Ally ran out.

"Hurry up," Kayla shouted. "Or we'll be late for the horses."

I didn't really think the horses would care, but we ran with them. We got to the corral in time to hear Bob, the horse trainer, tell everyone that the class was called horsemanship. "First, we will learn to saddle a horse. Then we'll see about mounting and directing them at a walk."

I nudged Luke. "Look who's here." It was Cody and Alan, looking like they thought horses were as boring as homework.

"First," Bob said to the group, "I'll introduce the horses. This little brown beauty is named Petunia. She's gentle and careful and dependable." He turned to a giant red horse. "This is Tiny."

Everyone laughed. "I'd hate to see what you call big," Luke shouted.

Bob laughed too. "You can see that Tiny was named before he grew up. He's gentle also." The next horse was jet black. "This is Blackjack. He's smart and fast and frisky. He knows all the tricks for getting rid of a rider. Don't get him going unless you know how to handle him."

He introduced the other horses. "Today we'll

begin to learn how to saddle and care for our horses. And if we have time, we'll hop on and take a short ride."

Bob and some of the other helpers showed us how to toss on the blanket first, then the saddle. I didn't like standing almost underneath Tiny to buckle it on.

"Get it good and tight," Bob warned, "or you'll find yourself riding on the side of the horse. On your way to the ground."

Finally, we were ready to try a short ride. Bob sat on his horse, a palomino named Paint, and showed everyone how to work the horse's gas pedal and brake with the reins. "No matter what you've seen on TV, never kick your horse in the flanks to make it go. You direct a horse left or right by pulling on that side of the reins. Now, how many of you have ridden a horse before?"

He started matching kids with horses they could handle. "I hope I get Blackjack," a voice whispered behind me. It was Ally. "I like horses. I ride them every chance I get."

"I haven't ridden much," I said. "I'll be happy with Petunia. Or maybe a nice fence post. My mom wanted me to sign up for the special riding class after supper, but it was full."

"I knew it would be," she smiled, "that's why

I signed up for it early."

Bob was helping campers get up on the horses' backs. He called it "mounting the saddle," and he wanted it done correctly. "Put your left foot in the stirrup, then set up and swing your right foot over. Then hold the reins until I say otherwise."

"Rats," Ally said as Bob helped Alan up on Blackjack. "I wonder if he's really ridden a lot like he said." She got another black horse, and I had no trouble getting up on Petunia.

"Today, there will be no running," Bob called from Paint. "We're just learning to walk. Use the reins to direct your horse, and stay in line."

As we started down the path, I followed Ally's horse. I heard Alan, ahead of us, making fun of Cody's horse. "What kind of nag is that? It looks old enough to die before we get back."

Cody didn't like it. "What good was it to give you that fast horse? You've never even been on a horse. If you were any good, you'd be at the front of the line."

Alan couldn't take that. "I'll show you. Watch this!" He kicked Blackjack with both heels.

"Whaanahehe!" Blackjack bolted straight up on his hind legs, then dropped down and took off like a shot. Alan was holding on for his life.

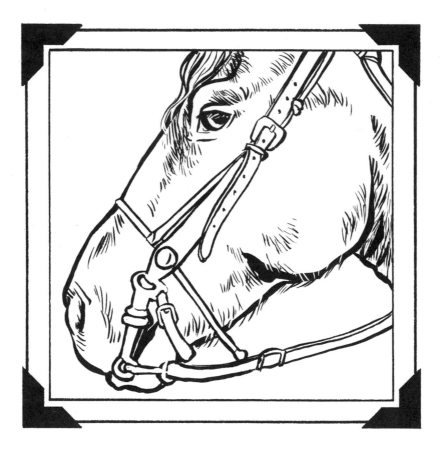

CHAPTER FOUR

Danger at the Corral!

Day Two

When Blackjack hit high gear, he flashed past the other horses like they were standing still. Alan was barely hanging on, bouncing from side to side in the saddle. Paint took off after them, almost before Bob clicked the reins and leaned forward.

Ally pulled up beside me. Her face was white. "They'll never catch Blackjack. Bob said he was the fastest horse here."

I don't think they would have. But Blackjack did something no one expected. Especially not Alan.

Blackjack stopped.

Alan flew over Blackjack's head and disappeared in the cloud of dust. Then Blackjack reared up! His hooves flashed in the air over Alan's head!

31

Suddenly, Paint was there. Bob jumped off and walked directly in front of Blackjack. He ignored the flying hooves and talked softly. "It's OK, boy. Settle down, now. Everything is all right." Bob protected Alan from Blackjack's hooves with his own body.

Alan didn't move. As Blackjack began to calm down, only tossing his head and whinnying loudly, Bob walked him back to the corral. There, he patted him a few more times, then turned him loose inside the fence. He whistled for Paint and motioned for Alan to come back in. "What happened?" he asked when Alan arrived.

"I didn't do anything," Alan started to say. Ally almost jumped out of her saddle.

"Not anything? Then why did the horse run?" Bob asked.

"Well, maybe I kicked him a little," Alan mumbled.

Bob went through the roof. Well, he would have, if there had been a roof! "You kicked him? After what I said? No, you probably weren't even listening. Do you know that that horse could have killed you?" By now, Bob was right in Alan's face.

Alan stared at the ground. The rest of us looked away like we were actually trying to decide if it would rain. I felt bad for Alan, even though Bob was right and Alan deserved it.

The rest of the class went by very quietly. Alan got another horse—a sway-backed old nag that probably hadn't run since the year Alan was born.

At supper, Mr. Morgan walked by our table. He glared at Luke, who had three hot dogs on his plate. "I'm eating them, sir," Luke said, stuffing a whole hot dog in his mouth at once.

Some people couldn't do that. Luke did it, and never stopped talking. It was amazing to see. And gross.

But seeing Mr. Morgan reminded Kayla of something. "Zack! Something strange happened in the kitchen this morning. Ally, you tell him."

She talked between bites. "I was cleaning out the big serving pans—you know, the ones that hold the biscuits and stuff that never got served. Anyway, I started to dump them in a trash can, but Mr. Morgan stopped me."

Kayla interrupted. "Stopped her? He shouted and got all huffy and told her to go on and sort the silverware." She waved a carrot stick around as she talked.

Ally ducked away from the swinging carrot and went on. "Right, and here's the strange part. He took those leftovers and dumped them in another trash can."

I shrugged. "So he's picky about his garbage."

"That's not the really strange part!" Ally stopped and waved a forkful of broccoli at me. "Will you let me finish?" She tapped my plate with the fork until the broccoli almost came off.

"OK, I'll listen. Just get that stuff away from me. Broccoli and I have this understanding. It doesn't eat me, I don't eat it."

"Sorry," she said. "This is the really strange part. He put the trash can in the refrigerator!"

Now, that was weird.

"Anyway," Ally sniffed, "I thought you might want to know. After all, that noise last night had something to do with trash cans, didn't it?"

"Yes. Of course. Thank you." I tried to be specially nice. Ally is the kind of girl who keeps her eyes open. The way things were going, I might need her help. Besides, I didn't want any more broccoli attacks. "Be sure to let me know if you see anything else suspicious."

She smiled. "I will."

Luke shook his head. "Putting garbage in the fridge is a very strange thing to do. What do you think it means?"

"I don't know," I answered. "What we have so far is this: garbage cans knocked around at night. Someone switching off the electricity. Money

missing in our cabin. And the cook keeping garbage cans in the refrigerator."

"What can all of those things mean?" Kayla
asked.

"I don't know," I said. "Only one thing we can
know for sure—someone is outside at night doing
something. And whoever it was came into our
cabin and stole Luke's money."

"I know who my first suspects are," Luke said,
rolling his eyes toward the Mohawk table.

"Or maybe that strange Mr. Morgan," Ally added.

Just then, Mrs. Carter blew her whistle. With
his hands over his ears, Luke said, "I wish someone would steal that thing."

Mrs. Carter talked about camp spirit and made
announcements. "Tomorrow, the Arapahos pick
up the trash, the Zuni cabin will help clean up
after breakfast, the Comanches have the flag-
raising and lunch clean up, and the Cherokees
help after supper."

There was a low moan from Luke and Max.

"The next day we'll begin our hiking trips to the
overnight camps. Your counselors will be telling
you more about them. Before you go, Wrangler
Bob wants to say something."

Bob looked smaller as he stood in the cafe than
he did in the corral. And he didn't seem dusty

enough. He cleared his throat and began. "Most of you have probably heard about our problem with a runaway horse this afternoon."

He waited while those who hadn't heard whispered questions to their friends. Then he went on. "Blackjack bolted because an inexperienced rider kicked him. We were very fortunate that no one was hurt. And it's a good lesson to all of us."

He turned toward Alan's table. Alan looked like he wanted to slide under his chair. "But I'm not here to talk about riding. I'm here to apologize to Alan."

If Alan's jaw fell open any more than mine did, it must have hit the table.

"I lost my temper this afternoon and yelled at Alan in front of everyone, so it's only right that I apologize in front of everyone. Alan made a mistake, a bad decision, and I was right to correct him. But it's never right to yell at someone after they know what they did was wrong."

The whole room was silent.

"Being a Christian means treating people like Jesus would, and I didn't do that this afternoon. I'm sorry, Alan, and I hope you'll forgive me."

A small voice came from Alan's table. "OK."

I thought what Bob did to save Alan from Blackjack was really something. But apologizing to him in front of everyone was really amazing!

Still, I guess Bob was right. Being a Christian means treating people like Jesus would. And Bob sure did that tonight.

I grabbed Luke's arm. "We're going to have to hurry to get set up before campfire."

Luke looked at me like I was crazy. "Get what set up?"

I wriggled my eyebrows. "No one's sneaking into our cabin tonight. We're going to set a trap!"

Clues About Christians

Bob risked his life to save Alan from Blackjack. That seems like a very Christian thing to do.

But apologizing to him was really treating him like Jesus would. Bob seems like someone who is different because he believes the Bible.

Thunder Mountain Mystery Clues

The cook is keeping some garbage cans in the refrigerator. Why would he do that?

CHAPTER FIVE

Petunia and the Good Samaritan

Day Two

"We need to catch whoever is coming into our cabin," I told Luke. "There may be a connection to the other mystery at the cafe."

"What will we do?" Luke asked. "Stay up all night and watch for them?"

"We can't do that," I said as we walked into the cabin. "That's why we have to set a trap." Max, Peter, and Brian crowded around.

"What trap?"

"What are we going to catch?"

I waved my arms. "Hold on, everyone. We have to think this through." I paced back and forth. "We know that someone came in during the night and took Luke's money. And the only way in here is through the door."

"Why couldn't they come through the windows?" Peter asked.

"The windows all have screens," I pointed out. "And the screens are latched from the inside. Even if the latch wasn't fastened, whoever crawled in would have to crawl across either your bed or Max's. Without waking you up."

"No way," Max said. Peter shook his head too. I went on.

"So whoever it was, came in through the door. And whoever was out there last night was probably at the cafe too."

I went over and opened the door, pulling it toward me. "What we need is something to wake us up if someone pushes the door open."

"What if we just block the door so it can't be opened," Brian suggested. "We could move Peter's bed in front of it."

"That would keep them out," I agreed, "but we wouldn't know who was doing it. Or if they had something to do with the kitchen mystery."

It was quiet for a moment. Then an idea hit me like a hammer. "Peter! You have soda pop in your suitcase, don't you?"

Peter nodded. "I used to have six cans. But now they're all empty."

"But do you still have the cans?" I asked.

Peter looked confused. "Of course. I collect them for recycling. I'm taking them home."

"Perfect!" I shut the door. "We'll take Peter's cans and stack them here in front of the door. Whenever the door opens, the cans will fall over, and the noise will wake us all up."

"Good plan!" Max shouted. Peter started digging the cans out of his stuff. I stacked them six-high, right next to the door.

"This is gonna be great," Luke said. "Nobody's gettin' in here again. I'll leave all my quarters out now." He waved a clinking little leather bag around.

"How many quarters do you have?" Peter asked. We all gathered around to look in his money bag. It was stuffed!

"Why would you bring so many quarters to camp?" Brian asked.

Luke looked down. "I thought there might be video games."

We were still laughing about that when the cans crashed over behind us.

"Whoa! They're here!" Max shouted, jumping for his bed.

"My quarters! They're after my quarters!" Luke cried. He crawled under his bed.

"What is going on?" Dave called from the doorway. "What are these cans doing here?"

"Dave," I sighed, collapsing on Luke's bed, "you scared us half to death."

"I can see that." He laughed as Luke crawled out. "But what are you doing?"

We told him about it—how Luke's money was taken, how we were setting a trap, and how we were going to catch the thief.

"Well, those cans will certainly tell you if someone opens the door. But don't you think that anyone who is trying to sneak in will hear the cans crash? And run?"

I hadn't thought of that. There would be no way to wake up and get out the door in time to catch them.

"Anyway," Dave said, "it's almost time for campfire. Let's not be late." We followed him down to the campfire bowl. I was still thinking about the trap. But the program gave me something else to think about.

After a few of our favorite loud songs, Mrs. Carter welcomed us all to campfire. "Are you having fun so far this week?"

"Yeeesss!" everyone shouted. The Mohawks didn't shout, but they were smiling.

"There is still a lot of excitement to go. Tomorrow, the first of the cabins will go on their overnight hike to Mountain Treehouse Camp." While she talked, the bushes behind her rustled suspiciously. We heard whispering.

Suddenly, off to one side, a kid in a wraparound robe-thing stepped out of the bushes. "Whoops," he said as he realized it wasn't time for him to show up. Everyone laughed.

Mrs. Carter went on. "I see they're ready. Tonight, the Arapahos have our program. They will be doing their skit, 'The Good Samaritan.' "

Greg, the Arapaho counselor, stood up. "It's important to remember that Jesus told the story of the Good Samaritan to answer a question: 'What do I really have to do to be a follower of God?' "

Greg left, and the same kid came back out of the bushes and walked by in front of us, whistling to himself and watching the sky as if he didn't have a care in the world. Suddenly, two guys rushed out, grabbed him, and threw him to the ground.

One of the Mohawks whispered, "Yeah! Why don't we get to do fun parts like that?"

The two robbers grabbed the traveler's bag, beat him with it, and then left him there, lying in the dirt.

Before long, someone all dressed up like a priest

came out. He looked at the body lying there and sniffed. "Someone really should help the man. I can't because I'm on my way to church." Then he hurried away.

Another Arapaho came out. He stopped to look at the traveler. "I'd better get out of here fast! Whoever did this might still be around. I'll report it to the police in Jericho."

Then someone walked by the front carrying a sign that read, "What we would expect the Samaritan to do."

Then Bob, the horseman, rode out of the bushes on Paint. He stopped when he saw the boy lying on the ground. Then he laughed and shouted, "Good! Another dirty Jew got what he deserved." He threw something at the body and laughed again. Then he rode away.

The sign boy came back. This time the sign said, "What the Good Samaritan did."

When he was gone, the Arapaho counselor came out of the bushes, riding Petunia. When he saw the traveler's body on the ground, he stopped and picked him up and put him on the horse.

"Oof," the boy grunted when he was thrown across Petunia's saddle. Everyone laughed when Petunia turned her head to look at him like she was saying, "Are you all right?"

They took him to a place by the fire where he was cared for. At the end of the skit, Pastor Mike came up. "So Jesus asked, 'Who was that man's neighbor? Who truly cared about him?'"

"Petunia did," someone called out.

Pastor Mike laughed. "You saw what the Samaritan could have done. The Jewish man was his enemy. But he was a true follower of God—not like those who pretended to be followers by doing religious things."

He looked around at each of us. "What I want this skit to teach you is that being a follower of God will make you different. It will make you care about everyone, not just your buddies or cabin mates."

I've been thinking about how people should be different if they are real Christians. But I haven't thought about myself. Am I a real follower of God? Or am I just pretending?

Clues About Christians

  The Good Samaritan was good because he was a follower of God. That made him act differently than other Samaritans would act.

_____

_____

_____

_____

_____

_____

Thunder Mountain Mystery Clues

  A trap will catch the sneaky thief. If we can figure one out.

CHAPTER SIX

Trapped!

Day Three

You'll never believe what happened last night. "You know the problem," I told the guys. "We need to wake up when someone opens the door, but do it quietly so we don't scare them off, right?"

"Right," they agreed.

"Luke, didn't you tell me your mother made you pack a kite?"

"Yes," he grumbled, "she thought this might be a good place to fly a kite. I tried to tell her it was in a forest."

"But did she pack in some kite string?" I asked.

"Yeah. A big roll of it. You want it?"

I nodded. "I have a plan." Luke gave me the string. "Peter, lie down on your bed like you were sleeping." He laid down with his arms behind his head.

"Now, take off your shoes." Peter looked at me, but untied his shoes and dropped them on the floor. "And your socks."

When his socks were off, I demonstrated my plan. "See, I tie a string to the doorknob like this. Then, I tie the other end of that string to Peter's toe. Like so." I looped it around the big toe of his right foot.

"So when the door opens, it pulls his toe. And he wakes up!" Max was catching on.

Peter wasn't so sure. "How hard would it pull? Would it hurt?"

"I'm sure whoever opens the door will open it slowly," I answered. "And we'll tie one of those slip knots the way we learned in crafts today. You know, the kind the teacher told us not to make because they would just slip apart."

"Yeah," Luke agreed, "every one I made yesterday came apart. That's why the wallet-thing I'm making looks like spaghetti."

"Let's try it," I said. While Peter lay still, I opened the door slowly. The string tightened and pulled, then came loose from his toe.

"It works!" Peter said. "I would have woken up for sure."

Brian wasn't convinced yet. "But then what happens? What does Peter do if someone comes in and he wakes up?"

"Yeah." Peter suddenly frowned. "If I shout, whoever it is will run out."

I snapped my fingers. "Of course! We'll set up a tug system."

"A tug what?" Max asked, scratching his head.

"A tug system," I explained. "We'll tie a string from Peter to you, then one from you up to Brian."

Luke caught on. "Then a string goes from Brian to you and then one down to me. It's a great idea!"

"Maybe you'd better say it again," Max said. "Why do we all need to be tied down with strings?"

"Not tied down," I said, "tied together. See? When the door opens, it wakes Peter. He pulls on his other string to wake you up."

"Then I'll pull on my string and wake Brian up." Max was getting it. "And Brian's string will wake you and then Luke."

We agreed that when Peter felt the tug, he would pass it on, then count to ten. Then he would hit the light switch. We would all jump up and face the thief together.

It was kind of weird going to sleep with strings on two fingers. This time, we waited until Dave was in bed before we set our trap. So when a tug woke me up later, I knew the trap was sprung.

I laid there with my eyes closed, smiling. Because I was sure that the guys were all awake, just waiting for Peter to flip on the light. Then finally, we would have our thief.

But I didn't hear any other noises, and the light didn't come on. Finally, I sat up and found two problems with my plan.

First, no one was awake. Second, I could tell no one was awake because it was already getting light. I lifted my hand to look at the string and wonder what went wrong.

"Hey, stop pulling my arm," Luke mumbled. I leaned over to look and that woke up Brian.

"What? Who's . . . what?" Brian woke up slowly. He rubbed his eyes, which pulled on Max's string. Max woke up a little and stretched. That yanked Peter's hand.

"Yeow!" Peter cried. Without opening his eyes, he sat straight up and flipped on the lights. The rest of us just blinked at him. Finally, his eyes opened. "Did we get 'em?" he asked hopefully.

Max groaned and rolled over. Or tried to. His string got tangled in his bed frame. Luke tried to get up, but his string got caught on the sleeping bag's zipper. On the other side of the room, Dave woke up and looked at us.

"You look like something a spider drug in," he said. "Let me guess. Another trap?" We nodded.

"Well, I can see who it caught."

Max ripped the string off his finger and threw it at me. "The next time you have a bright idea, go fly a kite!"

When the trumpets got us up later, Dave said, "Hey, have you guys seen my watch? You know, my silver Mickey Mouse watch? I'm sure I left it right here by my bed."

So not only was my trap a real flop, but somehow, someone got in and took Dave's watch. It was a disaster of a morning. And guess who was all bright and cheery at breakfast.

"Isn't this a beautiful morning?" Kayla said as she sat down. "I wish every day started just like this."

I tried not to hit her with my fork.

"Did you hear about the horses?" Ally asked. "Bob thinks someone was in the corral last night. He thinks someone may have been riding Blackjack."

"Well, we know it wasn't Alan anyway," Luke laughed. "I don't think he'll get anywhere near Blackjack."

Kayla shook her head. "Don't be too sure about that. I heard that Alan is taking those special riding lessons every evening after supper."

"No way!" I said. "I know there weren't any

more openings for lessons. I wanted to sign up, but they were full. You're taking those lessons, Ally. There wasn't any room left, was there?"

Ally stared at her food. "No, there wasn't."

"Bob said the only way anyone else could take lessons was if someone dropped out." I stabbed my hash browns. "And I'm sure no one would do that."

Ally didn't say anything. But Kayla did.

"Didn't you tell me last night that you quit those lessons?" she asked Ally.

Ally looked at her and then at me. "OK. I told Bob I would drop out of the special riding class if Alan wanted to take it."

"Why?" I asked. "You told me how much you like riding. And how much you don't like the Mohawks."

Ally shrugged her shoulders. "I already know how to ride. He probably never had the chance to learn." I just looked at her. "So I was trying to be nice," she said. "So sue me!" Then she threw her toast at me.

I didn't say anything, but I was impressed. She gave up horse-riding just to help someone else. Someone she didn't even like. It kind of reminded me of the Good Samaritan.

Then I remembered why we were talking about horses in the first place. "Why does Bob think someone was in the corral last night?" I asked.

"Blackjack was out in the field instead of in the corral. I guess Bob doesn't think Blackjack could get out there without some help," Kayla answered.

I slapped my hand on the table. "We'll go there right after supper to look for clues."

"No, we won't," Luke said, through a mouthful of eggs. "We have cleanup duty after supper."

I was afraid that we wouldn't get to work on any clues today. Boy, was I wrong.

Clues About Christians

Ally showed that a Christian who believes what the Bible teaches really will be kind to people who aren't nice.

Thunder Mountain Mystery Clues

Our trap was a flop.

Dave's watch was taken from our cabin last night.

Someone may have been messing with the horses last night.

CHAPTER SEVEN

Tracks and Trails

Day Three

"What do these tracks tell you?"

Luke bent down close to the ground. "I don't hear anything."

Cindy laughed. "OK, smart guy, out of the way."

Cindy is our teacher for the track-and-trails class. "In this class, we will learn to identify animal tracks and trails in the wild," she told us. "We will also learn about marking a trail for someone else to follow."

She took us out to the lake and pointed out some tracks on the shore. "Even though Luke can't hear them, these tracks do tell us a lot. These are the tracks of a raccoon. You can see that he walked into the water here, then came back to the shore."

We followed the trail of the raccoon along the shore as Cindy told us more about tracking animals. "You can often read a whole story from the tracks. But you have to look closely, and pay attention to what you see."

She pointed to a set of smaller tracks away from the water. "What can you tell about this animal?"

I looked closely. "Well, it's a small animal. It had little claws that dug into the sand."

"And what does this mark tell you?" she asked, pointing to a line that sometimes showed in the sand between the footprints.

I thought about different small animals and how they walked. Then it hit me. "It's a tail! The animal had a long tail that sometimes dragged on the ground behind it."

"Right," Cindy said. "These are the tracks of a wood rat, or pack rat, as it's sometimes called. Now look, see how the tracks change here?"

Brian bent down this time. "The claws are digging in deeper. The back part of the footprint is missing. It started running. The front of its feet dug in deeper, like ours do when we run."

"I wonder what it was running from," Max said. "Maybe the raccoon?"

"No," Cindy stated, "the raccoon wouldn't be hunting a rat. Let's follow the tracks and see if we can learn anything else." We followed her, bent low to look at the tracks. Suddenly, she stopped.

Luke bumped into her. I bumped into Luke. Max bumped into . . . well, you get the picture.

"Ow!"

"Watch it!"

"Wait!" Cindy held out her hand. "Look at this!"

We poked our heads out past her arm and stared at the ground. There were more tracks and marks, but I couldn't tell anything from it.

"All the tracks are messed up," Max said. "You can't tell anything from that."

"Don't be too sure," Cindy said with a smile. "Look closely, and pay attention to what you see."

I looked again. The rat's tracks were headed straight toward a patch of briers. IIe was trying to get away, but from what? There were no other tracks beside his.

I looked at Cindy. She smiled but said nothing.

Right before the briers, the tracks were messed up. The dirt was kind of dug up, like someone had scratched it up with a stick. What could chase a rat without leaving tracks but scratch up the dirt? I tried to picture it in my mind. Suddenly, it snapped in place like I had pushed a button on the TV remote and found the right channel.

"It was a bird! An owl, I bet!"

Cindy clapped her hands. "Exactly! Probably a great horned owl. Look at this—the rat was running for his life here," she pointed to the tracks, "and here the owl struck. See where his claws raked the ground?"

Everyone got close and followed her story.

"But the owl missed. See where its wings beat the ground here? And here?"

We could see how the dirt was brushed back.

"And look at this. These leaves and twigs on the brier bush were broken. The owl must have been angry about missing dinner and pounded at the bush with its wings."

I let out a breath I didn't know I was holding. We all looked around as if the owl might be lurking in a tree nearby, still in a bad mood.

Cindy stood and looked at us all. "See what you can learn when you pay attention to what you see?"

Boy, did I!

That night, at supper, we told Kayla and Ally about the owl and the other things Cindy had taught us. "She told us how to mark a trail so someone could follow."

"What do you do, carve an arrow in a tree?" Ally asked.

"No, that might damage the tree," Luke explained. "You can show the way to go by using sticks—like this." He stuck the end of his knife into his mashed potatoes and then leaned it between the tines of his fork. "See? That points the direction of the trail."

Kayla said, "I see," and shuddered as Luke licked the mashed potatoes off his knife.

"Or," Luke went on, "you can mark the trail with rocks. A little rock on top of a big rock"—he put a green pea on top of the mashed potatoes—"means the trail goes straight. If the trail turns, you put another rock on the side it turns toward." He put another pea on the right side of his potatoes, as if his trail was turning toward Kayla.

"Let's go," I said. "We get to help clean up tonight."

"Ug," Luke grunted. "What's our hurry?"

I slapped his back. "Clues, man, clues. We're going to pay attention to everything we see in that kitchen tonight."

Kayla pointed to Luke's plate. "You'd better clean your plate. I wouldn't want to be in your shoes if Mr. Morgan sees you throwing away good food."

Luke glanced around like he was really afraid, then began stuffing everything into his mouth at once. The girls said, "Ooh, yuck!" and left quickly. I went to the kitchen.

"I'm here to help," I called as I opened the door.

DETECTIVE ZACK

Mr. Morgan said, "You can start on the pots. Spray them off in the sink. Then we'll run them through the dishwasher."

I tried to keep an eye on everything while I washed. I noticed one thing quickly. While Mr. Morgan wasn't exactly friendly, he wasn't mean either. When someone didn't understand, he explained it carefully until they did. He didn't shout or make fun of anyone. I guess I was expecting him to be different.

"See anything yet?" Luke whispered as he went by carrying a bag of trash.

"Not yet," I answered. "I'm trying to watch what happens to the leftover food. Look!"

Someone had started to empty the food pans, and Mr. Morgan stepped up. "I'll take care of that. You get the broom, and start sweeping the dining room."

I raised my eyebrows and nodded at Luke. I would keep watching. But, wouldn't you know it, I got busy spraying one big pot, and when I looked again, the food pans were gone.

When my pots were done, I saw Mr. Morgan helping a kid stacking plates for the dishwasher. *This is my chance*, I thought. I walked back toward the refrigerator and looked around. *That extra food must be around here somewhere.*

Then I heard something strange. It was a knocking sound, but it seemed very far away. I moved toward it. The noise was coming from the refrigerator. It sounded like someone was locked inside!

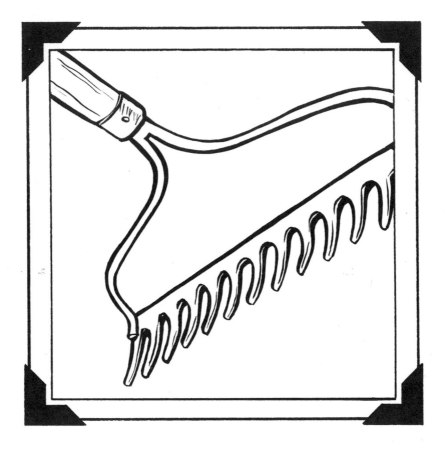

CHAPTER EIGHT

Clues in the Sand

Day Three

I grabbed the handle and swung the door open. There, next to the big can of potato salad, was Luke!

"T-t-thanks," he said through chattering teeth. He rubbed his arms to get warm. "The door locked behind me. I thought I was stuck for the night."

I looked at the inside of the door. "Did you push the handle release button?" I asked.

"What? I tried to push the handle, but it wouldn't go down."

I pointed to the sign on the door that said in big red letters: "Push Handle Release Button to Open Door." An arrow pointed to a big red button.

Luke just stared. "Oh. I guess I didn't see that."

I grabbed his cold arm. "Let's get out of here before Mr. Morgan shows up." We ducked out the back door of the kitchen and sat in the sun. Once we were outside, I asked the question I had been saving. "What were you doing in the refrigerator, anyway?"

Luke sniffed. "I saw Mr. Morgan carry some garbage bags in there. So I waited until he was gone, then snuck in to see what was in the bags."

"So? What was it?"

He kicked at the sand under our feet. "I don't know. As soon as the door shut, I forgot about the bags. Now we'll never know."

The sand gave me an idea. "Maybe we can still find out something. Come on; let's go ask Mrs. Carter for a rake."

We found Mrs. Carter at the camp office. "What can I do for you, gentlemen?" she asked.

"Can we borrow a rake?" I asked. "We want to do a specially good job of cleaning around our cabin tonight."

"Certainly you can. I like to see campers who take an interest in keeping their areas clean. Take one of the rakes leaning against the back of this building. You will bring it back tomorrow, won't you?"

"Yes, ma'am," I answered. We found a rake next to some cement blocks and dashed back. Everyone was gone by then. The cafe was dark, and the back door was locked. The evening's trash cans were lined up along the back wall. "Perfect!"

"Are we through running yet?" Luke asked, still panting.

I laughed. "We are ready to set our trap." I got busy. "I'm going to rake the sand in front of the door and trash cans all nice and smooth. That way, whoever comes here during the night will leave clues behind."

Luke was catching on. "Footprints! They'll leave footprints, and we'll be able to track them."

"Exactly," I answered. Soon, the ground was ready to collect clues, and we were ready to go.

"Wait a minute," Luke said as we headed back, "you told Mrs. Carter that we were going to rake around our cabin."

I grinned at him. "We are. That's the other half of our trap. We'll rake around our side of the cabin and around the Mohawks' side."

"That sounds like a lot of work."

"But look, this way we get clues on both mysteries. We'll know if the Mohawks leave their cabin. And we'll know if they come to our side."

Luke began to see the plan. "By the footprints. Right!"

I went on. "And the bonus is, if their footprints at the cabin match footprints going to the cafe, we'll know who's been down there too."

Luke was ready to dance a jig. "I like it! I can't wait to tell the guys."

I grabbed his arm. "Let's not tell them. After the way the last trap worked, I'd rather wait until we catch someone." He agreed to keep it a secret.

When we got to the cabin, the Cherokees were in an uproar.

"It happened again!" Max shouted.

"What?" I tried to ask. "What happened?"

Brian answered. "Some of Max's money was stolen. He left it on the floor while we went to supper, and now it's gone."

Max stopped stomping around and explained. "After swimming, I stopped by the camp store and bought these granola bars. My change was three dollar bills and a fifty-cent piece. I've never had one of those before, so I was going to keep it."

"So where is it?" Luke asked.

"I was late for supper, so I ran up here to change. I just left my money on the floor by Brian's bed. When I got back after cleanup, this was all that was left!" He waved the three dollars in our faces.

Something seemed strange to me. "Why would someone come into our cabin, steal fifty cents, and leave three dollars?"

"I was wondering that too," Brian said. "If

someone was looking for money, they'd take it all. Wouldn't they?"

Luke told everyone we were going to rake outside to get a head start on tomorrow's inspection. And that was true. Our cabin would look great with the yards all raked smooth. We took turns raking a wide section of the dirt around our side. When we started raking in front of the Mohawk side, their door opened.

"What are you doing?" Cody asked. For once, his voice didn't sound mean, just curious.

"We're raking," I answered.

Luke added, "Just trying to be neat and clean."

Cody didn't believe that. "You in some kind of trouble? And this is your punishment?"

"No," I answered. "We're getting a head start on inspection tomorrow."

"Then why are you raking our side?"

"Just trying to be friendly?" Luke suggested.

For a minute, I was afraid he would catch on to our plan and tell us to leave their side alone. But he rolled his eyes and went back inside.

"We'll have to be the last ones in tonight, so we can smooth out the last footprints after campfire," I whispered as we finished.

Luke smacked his forehead with his hand. "Campfire! The Hopis are doing tonight's skit.

Hurry, or we're going to be late!"

The Hopis did the story of Zacchaeus. Kayla was dressed up in a rich purple robe. At her house, by the front row of benches, there was a table set with a white tablecloth and glass dishes. She strutted around, taking money from other Hopis who were sitting on the ground, eating from old paper plates and dressed in dirty old clothes.

Then someone walked by, wearing a big sign around her neck. It was Kayla's friend Holli. The sign read "Jesus is coming!" Kayla's eyes got really big, the way they do when she sees a spider. She paced back and forth as if she didn't know what to do. Then she started to go to her right. Holli tapped her on the shoulder and turned around. A sign on her back read, "No, that way!" and pointed to the left.

We laughed.

A crowd of people (really, it was four or five Zunis who were helping the Hopis) came out of the woods from the left. Kayla rushed up to join them, but somehow, she was always behind them. They were taller, so she kept trying to jump up and see past them.

Finally, she gave up and ran to a tree. Climbing up to the first branch (not too easy in a robe), she sat and waited. Soon, someone in a white robe, wearing a fake brown beard, walked up and stopped under the tree.

I wasn't sure who it was until I heard her voice. "Zacchaeus, come down. I'm going to your house for dinner." It was Ally!

They went to sit at the table with the white cloth and pretended to eat. Kayla pretended to listen, while Ally pretended to talk. Pastor Mike stood up to speak.

"We're not sure what Jesus said to Zacchaeus, but the Bible tells us that Zacchaeus changed. That same night, he offered to give half of all he owned to the poor and to repay the people he had cheated with four times as much."

Kayla got up and took bags of paper money to the poor people still sitting on the ground. She threw handfuls in the air, and they grabbed for it.

Pastor Mike went on. "Zacchaeus wasn't rich anymore, but now he was happy. One thing always happens when a person decides to become a follower of Jesus. That person is always happier. And more fun to be around."

I'd never thought of it that way.

On the way back to the cabin, Luke grabbed my arm. I almost dropped my flashlight. "Trouble!" he hissed as he pointed.

I looked. There was a light on in the kitchen!

CHAPTER NINE

Confusing Clues

Day Four

"Quick! Let's go." Luke and I raced toward the cafe as fast as we could in the dim light of dusk. I didn't turn on my flashlight. We circled around to the back side and tried to peek in the kitchen windows.

"It's Mrs. Carter," Luke whispered. We could see her walking through the kitchen.

"What is she doing?" I wondered out loud. She seemed to be looking for something. "Hey, maybe she thinks something strange is going on too."

The light clicked off. I ducked down behind a bush. "Quick, get down. She'll see us."

"Not my dark skin," Luke whispered as he watched the back door open.

"Lucky," I muttered from the ground. Mrs. Carter stepped out with her flashlight shining around at the trash cans. She stood still for a moment, then walked away toward the camp office.

"We'd better go to the cabin and get the rake," Luke said.

"Wait, let's look first." I turned on my flashlight and traced Mrs. Carter's steps through the sand.

"Only one set of footprints," Luke said.

"She must have come in through the cafeteria doors," I said. "Look, her shoe print is kind of small, and it has crisscross lines. We'll know which prints are hers tomorrow morning."

Back at the cabin, we made a last-minute trip to the bathroom so we would be the last ones in for the night. I raked the last prints from in front of the Mohawks' door very carefully. And quietly.

"How are we going to wake up before everyone else?" Luke whispered when the lights were out.

"Don't worry. I have a plan," I whispered back. I wasn't worried. Every morning of camp so far, my blue jay friend had returned to shriek at the top of his beak. I don't know about anyone else, but it woke me up every time. Before, I wasn't happy about being woken up at sunrise, but this time, it was going to work out fine.

"Screeeak!" My blue-feathered alarm clock was right on time. I hopped down and woke up Luke. "Let's go," I whispered.

Confusing Clues

We snuck out the door just as the sun was coming up. "Walk out away from the cabin so we don't mess up any tracks," I reminded him. We circled our side.

"I don't see anything," Luke said after a minute. "Wait, here's something." I bent down and looked close. "It's a wood rat's tracks, just like the ones we saw yesterday. How about that! A wood rat visited our cabin."

"We don't have time for rats," Luke hissed. "Let's go around to the Mohawk side."

There, in the smooth dirt, were two sets of footprints, leading away from the door. Obviously, two people had left that cabin. I looked at Luke. "Paydirt. Quick, to the cafeteria."

What we found there was a complete surprise. "What on earth are those?" Luke asked. I knelt down to look closer. Mrs. Carter's prints were still there, but leading up to the door was something else, something bigger.

"They're horse tracks!" I exclaimed. "Look, they go right up to the door. The horse was walking slowly. See? The tracks are very clear. The sand around them is not disturbed much. Wait a minute, I've found more footprints."

We looked closer. "Someone got off the horse and walked to the door," Luke pointed out.

"Are those footprints the same as the ones at the Mohawk cabin?" I asked.

"I can't remember for sure. Let's go back and see," Luke said. "We'd better hurry. People are starting to get up."

Before we got to the cabin, I heard a door slam. I knew we were sunk when I heard Cody's voice. "Come on, guys. Let's get the showers first."

When we got there, the dirt in front of their door was stomped on by at least four pairs of bare feet. The shoe prints were gone.

"Rats," Luke said. "Well, at least we still have the prints down there."

I looked past him to the milk delivery truck coming up the road. "Not for long, we don't." We watched while it backed up to the kitchen door, destroying all the tracks there.

It was a big disappointment after all our trouble. Still, we had found an important clue. And something else we saw was tickling the back of my mind, but I couldn't quite remember what.

We did get a perfect score on our inspection anyway.

At horse class, we followed a new trail. As we walked our horses through the woods, I pulled Petunia up beside Ally. She was on Blackjack this time. I said, "Riding horses isn't so bad. It's easier than riding a camel."

Ally's eyebrows crawled to the top of her fore-head. "A camel?"

"I'd rather ride Petunia than Old Beauty any day," I said, remembering the knobby-kneed hump-back my friend Achmed and I rode. "On camels you go up and down and back and forth. It gets old fast. And then when they run! Ouch!"

Ally just stared. "You know how to ride a camel? And you're afraid of horses?"

I sat up straight. "I am not afraid of horses. I just prefer smaller animals—ones with less teeth and hooves. By the way, Bob was right about someone riding the horses at night."

"How do you know that?" she asked.

I told her about the tracks at the kitchen. "Someone rode a horse to the door and went in. I don't know what they're doing, but they're using a horse to do it."

"Have you told Bob?" Ally asked.

"No. I want to find out what's going on first."

We stopped the horses near a stream and got off to let them drink. "Hey, Zack," Ally called, "look over there." She pointed across the stream.

It looked like a big blue tent. "Why would a tent be out there by that farmer's field?" I asked. "Let's ask Bob."

When we asked him, Bob looked over at the tent and frowned. "I understand that a family lives there," he said.

"All the time?" I asked.

"In a tent?" Ally added.

He sighed. "The story is that they were homeless, and the farmer lets them live on the land while they work for him."

"Well, that's nice," Ally said.

Bob snorted. "I don't think the farmer is doing it to be nice. The camp gave them that old tent. Before that, they were living in their car. I think the farmer treats them like slaves. And he calls himself a Christian."

"Why don't you report him to the sheriff?" I asked.

He frowned again. "Then the family wouldn't have anywhere to live. Besides, Mrs. Carter has offered to help them, but they're too proud. They don't want our help."

Ally and I walked back to the bank of the stream. I was showing her animal tracks in the mud, but there weren't many that the horses hadn't trampled. We walked farther upstream.

There weren't as many horse tracks there, but one I recognized. "You can sure tell where Tiny has stepped," I laughed. "He's the only one big enough to make that print."

Ally looked around. "Zack, Tiny didn't come on this ride. He's back at the corral."

"Are you sure?" I looked around too. "He isn't here. But that has to be his print. Doesn't it?" I looked again. "It could look bigger because of the mud. Or maybe he was here last night."

Ally looked shocked. "Was it Tiny's tracks by the cafe?"

"I'm not positive. There were big tracks, but without other tracks to compare with, I'm not sure how big. But what if those homeless people are stealing things from the camp and using Tiny to haul them back here?"

Ally looked a little scared. "We'd better tell Bob."

"No," I decided. "Those people have enough trouble without us accusing them of being thieves if they aren't. Let's wait until we have proof."

When we got back to the camp, Luke was waiting. "Something else was stolen last night. Brian's silver whistle is missing."

Clues About Christians

  If a person says "I am a Christian" and then treats people like that farmer treats those homeless people, then, either the Bible isn't true—or else that person isn't really a Christian.

Thunder Mountain Mystery Clues

  Someone is using the horses to do whatever he or she is doing. The hoofprints by the cafe prove that.

  We saw a hoofprint that might have been Tiny's out by the stream. Could the homeless people be stealing food and using Tiny to haul it?

  Two sets of tracks left the Mohawk cabin during the night.

  No footprints led to our door. But Brian's silver whistle disappeared anyway.

CHAPTER TEN

Tracking Down
a Thief

Day Four

At supper, Luke and I sat with Kayla and Ally
at the corner table. We wanted to discuss the
mystery without other people overhearing us.

"First things first," Ally said. "What do we think
is going on?"

Luke answered. "We think someone is stealing
things—from the kitchen and from our cabin."

"I've heard about the missing things from the
cabin. Is anything missing from the cafe?" Ally
asked.

That puzzled me too. "I haven't heard of anything," I said, "but Mrs. Carter was searching
around last night. And Mr. Morgan acts suspicious of everyone. It could be that things are

missing, but they aren't telling us."

"Someone has been down here twice," I said. "The first time, when they knocked over the trash cans and then when they turned out the lights . . ."

"How'd they do that, anyway?" Luke asked.

"The breaker switches for the electricity are in that shed over there," I said, pointing to a small building between the cafe and the office. "Dave told me that's where they had to go to turn them back on."

I went back to what I was saying. "The second time was last night. We saw the footprints and hoofprints."

"We also saw footprints coming out of the Mohawks' cabin," Luke said.

"And don't forget the hoofprint at the stream," I added.

Ally started counting on her fingers. "So our suspects are the Mohawks, Mr. Morgan, or those homeless people."

I sighed. "Or it could be someone we haven't thought of."

"It does leave a lot of questions with no answers," Kayla agreed. "Like, is anything really missing from the cafe?"

"And, why would Mr. Morgan take anything?

He doesn't want any little thing to be wasted."
Ally wondered.

"And, why are things missing only from our cabin?" I asked.

Luke had to join in. "And, why don't we ever get ice cream for dessert?" We glared at him. He ducked down like we might throw things. "Well? Don't you wonder about that?"

Ally ignored him. "Are you sure nothing is missing from other cabins?"

I nodded. "I haven't heard of any. And what has been taken from us and what hasn't is very strange."

"What do you mean?"

While Luke explained about Max's fifty-cent piece being taken and his three dollars left, the back of my mind started tickling again. I thought about what had been taken—the coins, the watch, the whistle. Something about it . . .

"That is weird," Kayla was saying.

"It's like someone is starting a collection," Luke agreed.

Click. "That's it!" I shouted.

"What'd I say?" Luke ducked down again.

I grabbed him. "Luke, get the Cherokees together at the cabin. I'll meet you there in ten minutes."

DETECTIVE ZACK

Ally asked Kayla, "Does your brother get like this often?"

I didn't bother with them. I ran to find Cindy.

Ten minutes later, all the Cherokees and Dave arrived at the cabin. Kayla and Ally came too. Cindy, our tracking teacher, and I were waiting.

"We've all been wondering who's been taking our stuff from the cabin," I said. "Well, I found the thief."

"Cindy took our stuff?" Luke asked.

"Shh!" everyone said.

I went on. "I figured it out when I realized what all the missing things had in common. They were all shiny."

Now everyone thought I had lost my mind. Except Brian. I could see the wheels turning in his head. "If you've got it all figured out, where is the stuff?" Max asked.

"Follow me," I said. We walked back behind the cabin to the edge of the woods. I stopped at a skinny old stump and looked at Cindy. She nodded. I kicked the stump over with one blow.

There, in a pile of leaves and bark, was a watch, two quarters, one fifty-cent piece, and a silver whistle.

"What? How?"

As the others grabbed their stuff, Brian figured

it out. "It was a pack rat—a wood rat—wasn't it? They like shiny stuff."

"That's right." I grinned. "Luke and I found its tracks this morning in the dirt by the cabin. When I figured out what was happening, I asked Cindy to help me track it back to its home."

"Way to keep your eyes open, Zack," Cindy said.

"That was great!" Max added. "No wonder our trap didn't work. We should've had a rat trap."

Dave laughed while he slipped on his watch. "So he was sneaking in every night and taking the shiny stuff. Good detective work, Zack."

Ally didn't say anything. But she looked impressed.

Kayla didn't care. "So what does this do to the rest of the mystery?" she asked as the others walked away. "What about the cafeteria and everything?"

I frowned. "Well, I doubt if a pack rat is riding one of the horses to the cafe and knocking over the trash cans. So, something else is going on. We'll have to . . ."

"I know," she said in a tired voice, "keep our eyes open."

That night after campfire, we settled in—after we carefully packed all our shiny things away. Dave had an announcement.

"I have some good news and some bad news," he said. "The good news is—you don't have to go to flag-raising tomorrow."

"Yaay!" we shouted.

"The bad news is—you don't have to because you'll already be up."

"Booo!"

"The good news is—we leave on our overnight hike to Thunder Mountain Treehouse Camp at sunrise."

"Yaay!"

"The bad news is—we have to eat sack breakfasts."

"Booo!"

Dave was having fun with it. "The good news is—Bob is carrying most of our stuff there with the horses."

"Yaay!"

"The bad news is—the Mohawks are going with us."

Silence. Not even a boo.

"Come on, guys. Their counselor hurt his knee water skiing. Mrs. Carter has assigned two of them to each of the other cabins. Cody and Alan will be with us the rest of the week."

Peter spoke up. "Isn't the overnight hike supposed to make everyone work together? Isn't it like an obstacle course? Don't we have to help each other just to make it to Treehouse Camp?"

"Yes," Dave replied.

"So how are we going to make it with them?"

"We'll have to try hard to work with them. We can make them feel like part of our team. Remember, we're the ones who claim to be on God's team. Isn't there room for Mohawks there?"

Everyone was quiet again. Then Brian said, "I'll try, Dave."

Luke and I said it at the same time. "Me too."

Peter echoed what we said. Finally, Max agreed. "OK, I'll try," he grunted.

I'm not sure what everyone else thought, but I hoped there wouldn't be any problems. *Whatever happens, I'm sure it won't be all that bad*, I thought as I drifted off to sleep.

Boy, was I wrong.

CHAPTER ELEVEN

The Trail to Treehouse Camp

Day Five

The trail to Treehouse Camp is tough! After a long hike uphill, we came to a narrow pass between two rock cliffs. Across our path was a wooden wall.

"What is that?" Peter asked.

"It's the flattest tree I've ever seen," Luke answered.

Dave laughed. "It's our first obstacle. We have to go over the wall."

"But it's taller than we are," Brian protested.

"That's what makes it an obstacle. You'll have to work together to get over it. And I can't help."

With that, Cody and Alan sighed and dropped their packs to the ground. "Get out of the way,"

Cody said, "I'll get over the wall." He ran at it and jumped as high as he could. His hand didn't reach the top, and he slid down to the ground.

After two more tries, he gave up. As he sat panting, Max said, "Now what do we do?"

I looked at the wall. "If we had some rope, we could . . . it doesn't matter, we don't have any rope."

Cody snorted. "If we brought a ladder, or if we were twice as tall, we could go over it too."

Brian's head popped up. "That's it! Twice as tall! What if we stand on someone's shoulders?"

Cody stood up. "Good idea, Brainy. Alan, come here." He bent down to make a foothold for Alan to step in. "You get up on my shoulders."

Alan stepped up onto Cody's handhold and put one foot on his shoulder. "Whoa! Hold still!" Alan swayed back and forth like he was going to fall.

"I'm trying!" Cody wobbled too.

"Here, hold my arm," I shouted, joining Cody. Alan grabbed my hand and steadied himself. Then he let go and stood up straight.

"Come closer to the wall," he said. Cody did, and Alan reached over and grabbed the top of the wall. He pulled himself up and away from Cody. We backed up to watch him pull up and sit on the top of the wall.

"Hey, after you get here, it's easy!" Alan called. "There's room to sit up here and the other side is like a long slide."

"Great," Max said, "but how do the rest of us get up there?"

"We'll have to do it the same way," I said. Cody looked at me. He was still rubbing his shoulders. "We'll take turns," I said to him.

Brian got up on my shoulders next. He stretched up but couldn't grab the top of the wall. Alan reached down and pulled Brian to the top. "OK," he called down, "that's one."

Cody helped Luke up next. Then I staggered around until Max grabbed the top. It took both Cody and me to get Peter up.

"You next," Cody said when we were the last ones left. I stepped up onto his shoulders and pulled myself up to the top.

"How do we get you up?" Alan asked Cody. Cody shrugged and got ready to run and jump again.

"Wait," I called, "I have an idea." I grabbed the top of the wall and hung down. "Max, you hold my arms. Cody, jump up and grab my belt."

Alan caught on. "I'll reach down and grab Cody and help him up past you. Come on, Cody, do it."

"I hope this works," Max muttered.

"I hope Zack's belt doesn't break," Luke said.

Cody caught my belt on the first try, and Alan had him up in a second. We waited while Dave jumped up and joined us. Then we all slid down the back side.

"Way to go," Dave said. "You guys really worked together."

Cody didn't say anything, but he smiled.

Our next obstacle was a stream. We had to cross it on a vine. "Aaaah!" Luke called like Tarzan as he swung over. The hard part was getting the vine back to the next person. After Max and Cody and I were across, Peter came next.

"Jump!" we shouted, as Peter got to our side. But he didn't let go of the vine. When he swung back out over the water, Max ran to the edge.

"I'll grab him when he comes back," Max shouted. "Somebody grab me."

When Max grabbed Peter's leg, Cody grabbed Max. They were still tilting toward the water, so I grabbed Cody. Finally, Peter let go and we all fell over backward.

I don't know who started it, but the next thing I knew, we were all laughing. Even Cody and Alan.

The rest of the guys got across with no problems. Before long, we came to our last obstacle. "I can see the treehouse," Brian called from in front.

"But we have to cross a bridge."

"What's the big deal? It's just a bridge," Max said as he moved past Brian. Then he stopped. "What's holding it up?"

We all stopped at the edge of the canyon. The treehouse was on the other side. It was only about fifty feet across, but both sides of the canyon wall were very steep. It wasn't too deep, but at the bottom was a fast-running river.

But the problem for us was the bridge. "It's a rope bridge," Dave said. "It's safe to cross, but you have to be careful. If it sways too much, you can tip over the edge and fall. Work together, and you can get across easily."

The bridge was made of ropes tied together. There were wooden slats along the bottom to step on and kind of a web of rope on both sides. A thick rope ran along the top of both sides like a handrail. "I don't think I like this," Brian said.

Dave gave us one bit of advice. "It's easiest if one person stands on each end to steady the bridge while the others cross."

"I'll go across first." I stepped out onto the wooden slats of the bridge and grabbed the ropes on both sides. The bridge sank down a little with each step. When I got out near the middle, the whole bridge started to sway from side to side. I stopped and took a deep breath. I looked down at the rushing water, not so far below.

"Keep going. You can make it," a voice called from behind me. It was Cody. He was standing at the end, holding the bridge steadier. I kept going. Before long, I got the hang of walking with the swaying, and it was easy.

"Come on," I called from the other side. "It's easy once you get used to it." With Cody and me on the ends, the others crossed without any trouble. I think Brian crossed with his eyes closed.

I waited while Cody started out. He figured out the swaying faster than I did, and almost ran across. "That was easy," he said as he reached my side. "Let's go across again."

But the others were calling from the treehouse. "Come on, this is great!" So we ran after them.

Treehouse Camp is the best! A rope ladder leads up the side of the enormous tree and into the treehouse. "This place is as big as our cabin," Max said. "And look how far you can see!"

We set up camp, and Dave built a fire in the pit under the tree. "This is the best meal we've had all week," Peter said. "Hand me another hot dog."

When the marshmallows were gone too, we leaned back and watched the stars come out. "We sure are lucky to be here at camp," Brian said.

"This is great."

I agreed. "I can't wait to tell Mom and Dad about this."

Cody snorted. "You guys have it so good. The last time I saw my dad, he punched me in the face."

What do you say after that? I looked at Cody a little differently. Maybe he wasn't just a tough, mean kid. Maybe he felt lonely. And afraid.

Brian felt bad too. "How did you get to come to camp, Cody?"

Cody stared at the fire. "The church people convinced my mom that camp would be good for me. I guess it has been. I mean, I haven't been in any trouble this week. At least, not like I would be at home."

Everyone was quiet for a few minutes, listening to the fire crackle. Then Cody said, "You guys are lucky to believe in God. It must be nice to really believe that someone cares about you and watches over you."

Dave spoke up. "You can believe in God too, Cody. He loves you more than you can imagine."

Cody just stared at the fire. Before long, the others began climbing up to their beds. I was part of the way up the ladder when I heard Cody mumble. "No one has ever loved me."

CHAPTER TWELVE

Lost on Thunder Mountain

Day Six

"We need to get started early today," Dave said the next morning. "There's a chance of thunderstorms this afternoon."

I was first over the bridge again. Dave followed me and sat on the edge of the canyon to watch. Everyone made it across again without trouble, with Cody and me holding the ends steady. Then Cody started across.

"Hey, watch this," he called from the middle of the bridge. He leaned to his left, then back to his right. The bridge started swinging back and forth.

"Cody! Cut that out and come on across," Dave called.

Cody rocked the bridge again, then started on

toward us. "I was just having a little fun," he said. His next step was just a little too far on the right side. The whole bridge tipped.

He grabbed the rope rail and held on for a second. But before I could do anything, Cody fell over the side and splashed into the stream below.

"Cody!" I shouted. I held on tight and leaned as far as I could over the edge of the bridge. Behind me, Dave dropped his backpack and jumped off the canyon wall. Everyone else rushed to the edge and looked down, shouting and screaming.

I watched Dave splash into the water and come up. He looked around for Cody. "Over there," I shouted. "He's down there by that log."

Dave swam down to where Cody was hanging onto a log at the river's edge. Together, they struggled up the bank nearest us.

The guys up on the wall shouted and cheered. I was still watching Dave, and he was trying to tell us something. "Hey, guys! Quiet! Dave's trying to talk."

With everyone quiet, we could hear Dave's voice over the sound of the water. "Zack, we don't have any rope, do we?"

"No," I shouted.

He looked around and said something to Cody. "Is Cody OK?" I asked.

"He hit his foot on a rock, but I don't think it's broken."

Luke shouted, "Dave, how are you going to get out?"

Dave looked at the wall above him and the rushing water. "I don't think we can. You guys are going to have to go back to camp and get help."

Luke looked at me. "Do we even know how to get back?"

I shrugged. "We can go back the way we came. But it took us all day to get here. That's too long for them to wait."

Dave shouted again. "Zack, you guys took tracks-and-trails class, didn't you?"

"Yes."

"There's a shortcut back to the camp from here. It starts at that big pine tree just down the path."

I turned to be sure I could see the tree he was talking about. The big tree was there in plain sight.

"OK," I shouted down at him.

"You should be able to follow the trail markers. If you get mixed up, remember the camp is down-hill. And, Zack, be very careful. Keep everyone together."

I stood up straight and walked over to the guys. "OK, you heard him. Let's go."

Alan took a last look over the ledge, then joined us as we started back down the path. At the big tree, Brian saw the trail first. "This way, Zack. See the marker?"

We started at the spot where a small rock sat on a larger one and followed that path for a long time. We turned when we found rocks that marked a turn to the right or left. Then Brian asked, "Do you think they'll be all right?"

"They're fine," I answered. "Dave said Cody was OK. They'll wait there on the bank until Bob or Mrs. Carter brings the horses and enough rope to pull them out."

It sounded great. Until we came to a place where the trail split. And right where the rock markers should have been was a fallen tree.

"What do we do now?" Max asked. I looked in both directions, but I didn't see anything that would help.

Alan spoke up. "Dave said to keep going downhill. That way seems more downhill to me." He pointed to the right.

"I think he's right," Luke said. It made sense to me, so we turned right. After about twenty minutes, we came out in a meadow, and the trail disappeared. We were completely lost.

"We need to go back to where we were," Peter

said. He sounded really scared.

"Go back where?" Max demanded, pointing behind us. "We have no idea where the path is."

"What can we do?" Peter whined. "We have to do something!"

I stepped in. "What we need to do first is calm down. We can't be too far from camp. We were on the right path for a long time."

We just sat and breathed for a minute. Then Luke said, "Someone should climb a tree and look around. They might see something helpful."

"Good idea!" Everyone liked that. We decided Luke would climb up. Before he did, Brian had another idea.

"I think we should pray," he said. "After all, this isn't just for us. We're trying to help Cody and Dave."

Alan raised his eyebrows. "Do you really think that will make any difference?"

"Alan," I said, "we really believe in God. We really think He cares about us. And about Cody. And you." I didn't know I believed it that much until I said it.

He looked at me for a second. "Then let's pray," he said quietly.

Brian prayed. "God, help us find our way back. You know that Cody and Dave need help. Keep them safe. Amen."

Soon Luke was calling from way up in a tree. "I see a larger clearing in that direction. It might be that farmer's fields you told me about."

We headed that way. I thought we might find a path back from there. I was stepping over a log when Brian shouted, "Stop!"

I froze with my foot in midair. "What is it?"

He pointed to the ground in front of me. "Hoof-prints!"

We all bent down to look. "They're big prints," I said. "They must be Tiny's. Which way are the tracks going?"

Everyone scouted around, careful not to cover any tracks. "This way," Alan called out from a sandy spot. "The tracks are going this way." I was headed over toward him when he shouted again.

"Wait a minute—the tracks are going both directions. See?"

Max looked. "He's right. Some of the tracks are going to the left, and some are going to the right. Which way do we go?"

I tried to pay attention to what I was seeing like Cindy taught us in tracks class. Finally, I saw it. "Look! The tracks going to the left cover over the tracks to the right."

"So?" Max asked.

"That means Tiny went that way," I said, pointing to the right. "Then he came back. He must have been heading back to camp. So we go this way—left!"

The guys cheered. I walked in front, slow enough to see the hoofprints. Luke walked beside me. "Why do you think Tiny was out this way?"

"I think I know, but we have other things to worry about now," I answered. "Have you seen how dark the sky is getting?"

Just then, we heard a little thunder behind us. I started walking faster. "That's real trouble," I whispered.

"You mean lightning?" he asked.

"Yes, but worse than that, rain. If it starts to rain, these tracks will wash away. Then how will we find the camp?"

Boom! This time, the mountain shook. "Well, now we know why they call it Thunder Mountain Camp," Luke said.

"Zack," Brian called from the back, "what will happen to Cody and Dave if it rains? Will that river flood?"

Suddenly, everyone was worried. "Not unless it rains very hard," I answered. While I spoke, we heard the first drops hitting the leaves above us.

"Let's hurry," I added.

CHAPTER THIRTEEN

Something Strange and Amazing

Day Six

We hurried as fast as we could follow the tracks. Then, between thunder claps, I heard something. "Wait!" I stopped and held out my hand.

"What? We don't have time to stop. Let's go!"

"Shhh!" I insisted. "Listen."

For a minute, all we could hear was the patter of the rain. Then, in the distance, ahead of us, we heard it.

"Attention, campers. Please stay inside your cabin until the storm is past."

Max jumped straight up. "It's Mrs. Carter on the camp loudspeaker!"

"I never thought I would be so happy to hear that voice," Luke shouted. "Let's go!"

DETECTIVE ZACK

Now we ran, following the sound. We raced right past the horses, past the cafe, and straight to the camp office. We hit the porch, sounding like a stampede. I jumped over a metal chair and slammed into the door. It popped open.

Mrs. Carter jumped back from the microphone. "What is going on here?" Bob jumped up from his chair as if he might have to throw us out.

"It's Dave and Cody," I panted. "They're stuck in the canyon under the rope bridge."

"What?" Bob asked. "Where's your counselor?"

"That's what we're trying to tell you," Max and Peter shouted.

"OK, OK, one at a time," Mrs. Carter said in a loud voice. "You," she said, pointing at me, "explain. Slowly."

"We were leaving Treehouse Camp this morning when Cody fell off the rope bridge. Dave jumped in after him."

Bob interrupted. "Are they OK? Did you see them?"

"They were OK. Dave helped Cody over to the riverbank. He said Cody's leg was hurt but not broken. But they couldn't climb out. The canyon walls are too steep. He told us to come back here and get help."

Five minutes later, Bob and two other counselors rode out through the rain with plenty of rope and a medical kit. We sat in the cafe and told Mrs. Carter everything that happened. Mr. Morgan brought us some hot chocolate.

By suppertime, the whole camp was talking about it. We were telling the story to Ally and Kayla when the horses rode up outside. "It's them!" Brian shouted.

Cody rode behind Bob on Paint. Dave followed on Tiny. "Boy, are we glad to see you," Luke shouted.

They hopped down, and Cody was hardly even limping. We all crowded around. "You're OK," I said to Cody.

"It's just a bruise," he said. "You guys saved us. We were starting to get worried when it took so long. Then when the storm hit . . ."

Alan interrupted. "We got lost. A tree covered the path markers, and we got turned around. But these guys figured out the way home."

"We did it together," I said. "But we were sure worried when the rain started!"

"So were we!" Cody laughed. "Especially when the river started rising. But Bob got there just in time. And Tiny pulled us out with no problems."

It was great to see Cody look so happy. I think he was beginning to believe that some of us really

113

cared about him.

After a few minutes of shouting and cheers, I finally got back to my supper and Ally and Kayla.

I told them how we found the way back. "After we prayed, we found these horse tracks. They were so big, they had to be Tiny's."

"But why would Tiny be going out that way all by himself?" Ally asked.

"Maybe it was a miracle," Kayla suggested.

"Maybe," I agreed, "but I think I know a way to find out for sure. And solve this mystery about the kitchen."

Before I could say any more, Luke ran up. "Zack! Come on, we still have the skit for campfire tonight. We have to practice!"

"See you later," I called back as I ran after Luke.

Our cabin's skit was the crucifixion of Jesus. We had agreed that Dave would be Jesus. He showed us the camp's wooden cross. "It fits into a hole by the campfire bowl. That way, you can make it stand up. And you can hammer these big nails into these holes here." He showed the holes to Cody and Alan, who were to be the Roman soldiers. "It will look real, and it gives me something to hold onto when you stand the cross up."

We practiced for a few minutes, but before long, we were waiting behind the bushes at the campfire bowl. The storm was over, and everyone wanted to sing. Finally, Mrs. Carter said, "Tonight's skit is 'The Crucifixion.'"

First, Peter played Pilate. "This man is not guilty. His blood is on your hands," he said. Then he washed his hands in a big bowl and walked away.

Next, Cody and Alan whipped Dave with grass whips. Dave acted like it was painful. He twisted and turned. When his back was toward the bushes, Luke squirted it with ketchup. "That looks real," Brian whispered.

"Too real," I agreed. It was kind of sickening. When Cody and Alan made Dave start dragging the cross toward the hole, the ketchup dripped and ran down his back. Dave dragged it part of the way, then collapsed into the sand.

Cody grabbed Max, who was standing nearby watching. "You! Carry the cross." So Max carried it the rest of the way, while Cody and Alan dragged Dave.

Brian and I, the disciples, followed them out and stood watching. When they laid Dave on the cross and pulled out those long nails, I thought about what really happened to Jesus. For the first time, maybe, I really thought about what Jesus did for me—to rescue me.

Cody stuck his nail in place and swung the big hammer. Blam! The cross shook, and Dave's arm twitched. Then Alan took a swing at his nail. Blam!

Max stood with us and watched. "We sure picked the right parts for Cody and Alan," he whispered. "They probably think being a Roman soldier is fun. I bet they 'accidentally' hit Dave's finger. Or do something strange."

I kept watching, and sure enough, Cody did something strange. Something no one expected. He stood up and threw the hammer down.

"I won't do it!" he shouted at Dave, with tears running down his face. "If Jesus was a person like you, He didn't deserve to die."

I couldn't believe my eyes. Cody walked over to the edge of the woods and sat with his head down. Alan dropped his hammer and joined him. No one else moved. I think everyone was in shock.

Finally, Dave stood up, dropped the cross in the hole, and walked over to sit next to Cody and Alan. Pastor Mike came up to the front. Everyone was silent when he spoke.

"Cody is right. Jesus didn't deserve to die. But He was willing to die to save us. To rescue us from the sadness of this world. The Bible says that He loved each of you enough to die so that you can live forever with Him.

"Are you willing to follow Him and let Him change your life? He will, and He'll make you a happier person. If you want to follow Him, stand up."

I was already standing up, but I stood straighter. I watched Cody and Alan stand up with Dave as Pastor Mike spoke again.

"You've heard me say that calling yourself a Christian and claiming to believe the Bible don't mean anything if your life isn't different. Remember the Good Samaritan and Zacchaeus?

"If you start following God, you are going to be different—happier, more kind and caring, and more fun to be around."

I looked over at Cody and shook my head. *It is amazing how much God can change a person in just one week*, I thought. *I guess the Bible is right again. Being a Christian really does make you different. If you let God change you.*

Pastor Mike paused and looked out at every face. "Jesus says, in the Bible, that when we're ready to show the world that we're going to follow God, we should do what He did—be baptized. If you're ready to tell the world that you're going to follow God, and let Him change you, then join me up here, and we'll talk about being baptized."

DETECTIVE ZACK

I was the first one there.

Later, on the way back to the cabin, Luke said, "This was the best camp ever. Nothing turned out like I thought it would. But everything turned out great."

"Not everything," I reminded him. "We still haven't solved the mystery at the cafeteria. But we're going to. Tonight. Come on, we have one more trap to set."

Clues About Christians

God did answer our prayer and help us find our way back to camp.

Cody was right. Jesus didn't deserve to die. But He was willing to, so He could rescue me.

I know that the Bible is true. If someone really is following God, that person is different—happier, more caring and kind, and more fun to be around.

I can see how much God has changed Cody in one week. I want Him to change me too.

I want to be baptized and tell the world that I'm really following God.

Thunder Mountain Mystery Clues

Tiny's tracks led us home. But where did he go out there? And who was riding him?

Tonight's trap has to work!

CHAPTER FOURTEEN

Mystery at the Cafe

Day Seven

"Grab your kite string again," I told Luke in the cabin. As we slipped behind the camp office, I snatched two of those cement blocks with holes in them that I remembered from before.

"Grab that chair," I whispered to Luke. He looked puzzled, but picked up the metal chair from the porch. By the time we got to the back door of the cafe, I was huffing and puffing.

The trash cans were lined up along the back wall, as usual. I grabbed the skinny bush that stood next to one end of the row of trash cans. "Help me bend this bush," I said.

"This is no time for bush-wrestling," Luke said. "What are you doing?"

"Look," I explained, "we're going to bend this bush back away from the trash cans. Then we're going to tie it there with your kite string. We'll run the string down through a cement block on this side of the doorway and then across to a block on the other side."

Luke got the picture. "So when someone walks through the back door, they'll trip over the string. It'll break, the bush will pop back up, and crash!"

I nodded with a big smile. "It'll sound like Thunder Mountain Camp, all right. Everyone will hear it."

We got the blocks in place; then I leaned on the bush while Luke tied the string. "OK," he said when it was all tied. I stepped slowly back, and the bush stayed bent. Perfect!

"By the way," Luke said, "what was the chair for?" But by then, I was carrying it around to the side. When I got back, he was busy hiding from two kids with a flashlight.

"Let's go before we get caught down here," he hissed.

The counselors let everyone stay up a little later, since it was the last night of camp. "Keep your flashlight handy," I told Luke. We had barely settled down when it happened.

Crash! Boom! Bang!

Everyone ran to the windows. "What was that?"

"Not another storm, I hope!"

"Is someone out there?"

By the time they stopped asking questions, Luke and I were out the door. As we ran from the cabin, I whispered to Luke, "Turn on your flashlight."

"Why?" he whispered back. "They might see us coming." Suddenly, all the lights in camp went out. Quickly, his light clicked on.

"That's why," I said. "Now, this way."

He wanted to run to the cafe. "They'll get away," he hissed.

"Not if we hurry." We rushed past the office to the little electricity building. Its door was open, so I shoved it closed, then reached for the metal chair I had leaned against the wall earlier. I wedged the chair under the door handle.

"Now what?" Luke asked.

"We wait," I said.

"Wait! What about the thief?" As he spoke, the door knob clicked back and forth. "Hey," he whispered, "someone's in there."

"I know."

Before we could talk anymore, Mrs. Carter came rushing around the corner. Her flashlight lit us up. "Zack! Luke! I'm surprised at you two. I didn't expect to find you out here turning off the lights."

"We didn't," I started to say. But then Bob dashed around the other corner. "What's going on?" he started to say. Then he heard a familiar whinny from the cafe. His flashlight found something very large. "What's Tiny doing out? You two have a lot of questions to answer."

"I think you should ask him," I said, pointing to the door. They watched while I moved the chair and opened it. "Come on out," I called into the darkness.

"I might as well turn the lights back on first," a voice said. With a click, the camp was lit up again. Then Mr. Morgan stepped out.

"Mr. Morgan! What is going on here?" Mrs. Carter was astonished.

"Well, I'm not sure I can say, ma'am," he answered.

"What do you mean?" Bob demanded. "You know something! And you can start by explaining why that horse is here."

Mrs. Carter gasped. "Are you stealing from the cafeteria?"

Mr. Morgan laughed softly. "I didn't say I don't know. I said I can't say. I promised I wouldn't. But no, I'm not stealing. You'll find nothing missing from the kitchen."

Before it got any worse, I spoke up. "Maybe I

can help. Mr. Morgan is using Tiny to carry left-over food to those homeless people at the farm next door."

Now it was Mr. Morgan's turn to look astonished. "How did you know that?"

I explained. "When someone knocked over the trash cans the first night of camp, and then the lights went out, I figured something was going on. Then Ally told me that you put the food that was cooked but not served in a special trash can. And put it in the refrigerator."

He sighed and nodded. I went on.

"I didn't put it together then, though. But Luke and I used that rake, Mrs. Carter, to smooth out the sand behind the kitchen so we could watch for footprints. We were surprised to find horse prints."

Bob shook his head. "I knew someone was messing with the horses."

"Then, I thought I saw one of Tiny's hoofprints in the mud at the stream by the farm. I wasn't sure. But when we were lost in the woods, we found a set of huge hoofprints going one direction and then back. I knew they must be Tiny's, and I hoped someone was using him to go away from the camp and return. It turned out I was right, because we followed them back to camp."

Suddenly, Mrs. Carter thought it through. "Zack,

how did you know Mr. Morgan would be here?"

I shrugged. "I thought he would want the left-overs from today. Luke and I set up a trap that would knock over the trash cans. I figured with all that noise, he'd do the same thing he did the first night—turn the lights off to keep you guys busy while he got away with Tiny. So I put this chair here where I could trap him. Then, all we had to do was get here before he got away."

Mrs. Carter didn't seem so mad now. She laughed a little. "Mr. Morgan, is all this true?"

Mr. Morgan sighed. "It's true. I promised I wouldn't tell anyone that I was bringing them food, but they need it so badly. Especially the babies. Still, I didn't take anything that wasn't going to be thrown away. I just hated to see it wasted when people were hungry."

I patted his arm. "I knew you weren't as mean as you pretended to be. Especially when you made us hot chocolate this afternoon."

He smiled at me.

"I'm sure we can work out something so you don't have to sneak food out at night," Bob said. "Boys, why don't you run back to your cabin now. And thanks for helping us clear this up."

We didn't tell anyone at the cabin about it. If Mr. Morgan needed it to be a secret, then it would be one. But we did have to tell Kayla and Ally the next morning at breakfast.

"That's why he put those trash cans in the fridge," Ally said. "He needed to keep the food fresh until he could take it to those people. I guess he really is a nice man."

Kayla shook her head. "Mom and Dad will never believe all the things that happened this week. Not even from you, Zack."

When I said goodbye to Ally, she said, "I'll see you here next summer, I hope!"

I kind of hope so too.

Luke said he would write. He doesn't live too far from me, so I might see him sometime.

When I told Cody goodbye, he grabbed my hand. "Thanks for being a friend, Zack." I hope he gets to find out more about following God. Knowing Pastor Mike, he will.

I think I learned a lot this week. People who really believe in the Bible, people who really follow God, are different. Even if they don't seem to be at first. Like Mr. Morgan.

I can tell Bobby that real Christians are different. And now I can tell him that I'm going to be a real Christian too. I feel pretty happy about that.

I guess it's true. Following God does make you happier. And it's a whole lot of fun!

DETECTIVE ZACK

The adventure series for kids that builds faith in the Bible!

Jerry D. Thomas

Each **Detective Zack** book is packed full of action and suspense as Zack collects evidence to prove the Bible is true and not a bunch of made-up stories.

Catch Zack in his latest adventure, **Danger at Dinosaur Camp**, when he tries to unravel the mystery of what really happened to the dinosaurs, while other campers keep seeing dino-shaped shadows in the canyon. What's going on? Get this and all the **Detective Zack** books today!

US$5.95/Cdn$8.65 each.

The Missing Manger Mystery (Book 5)
Paper. ISBN 0-8163-1234-6.

The Mystery at Thunder Mountain (Book 4)
Paper. ISBN 0-8163-1212-5.

The Red Hat Mystery (Book 3)
Paper. ISBN 0-8163-1169-2.

The Secrets in the Sand (Book 2)
Paper. ISBN 0-8163-1129-3.

The Secret of Noah's Flood (Book 1)
Paper. ISBN 0-8163-1107-2.

YOU GOTTA GET 'EM!

Available at your local Christian book store, or call toll free 1-800-44PRESS.